There's no such thing as a vampire!

With his heart beating in his throat, Spike looked around the general store. Breathless, he spotted his friends and hurried over to them.

"You're not going to believe this," he croaked.

"What?" asked Tulu.

"What?" asked the others.

"Violetta's a vampire!" Spike said. "A real vampire. I've got proof!"

A CANAL STREET KIDS BOOK

The Vampires Went Thataway!

by Nancy Lamb and Muff Singer

illustrated by Blanche Sims

little rainbow®
Troll

Published by Little Rainbow, an imprint and trademark of
Troll Communications L.L.C.

Printed in the United States of America.

10 9 8 7 6 5 4 3 2

Library of Congress Cataloging-in-Publication Data

Lamb, Nancy.
The vampires went thataway! / by Nancy Lamb and Muff Singer;
illustrated by Blanche Sims.
    p.   cm.—(A Canal Street Kids book)
Summary: The members of the Canal Street Club have a chance to
be extras in a vampire cowboy film.
    ISBN 0-8167-3950-1 (lib.)   ISBN 0-8167-3718-5 (pbk.)
[1. Vampires—Fiction.   2. Motion pictures—Production and direction—
Fiction.]   I. Singer, Muff.   II. Sims, Blanche, ill.   III. Title.
    IV. Series: Lamb, Nancy. Canal Street Kids book.
    PZ7.L16725Vam   1995   [Fic]—dc20   95-14844

For Rachel & Ryan,
and John & Kevin,
this one's for you—
with love!
   —N.L.

For Aimee and Alex
and, of course,
for Sarah—
forever and ever!
   —M.S.

With love,
to Mark.
   —B.S.

CHAPTER ONE

Frankie Stevens sighed romantically as she watched Johnny Waco take Belinda Blythe in his arms. Belinda closed her eyes, swooning as Johnny buried his mouth in her neck. Ever so slowly, he nuzzled her until he finally lowered her limp body to the couch. Then he turned his head.

Yes! thought Spike Piranna as he caught sight of the blood dripping from Johnny Waco's mouth. The Vampire Cowboy rides again!

Smiling, Johnny untied his red bandanna and wiped his mouth politely. "That's the best dinner I've had since that pretty little school marm," he said.

Spike grinned.

"Cut!" said Sylvia Kirk, the director. "Cut and print!" She flashed a thumbs-up sign to the two actors.

Clyde Perkins, the assistant director, raised his hands over his head like a Spanish dancer. Clap-clap-clap! The sharp noise captured everyone's attention. "Okay, everybody!" he called out. "Time to break for lunch."

Relieved that she didn't have to look at blood anymore, Tulu Stevens opened her eyes. Her older sister, Frankie, nudged Emily Anderson's arm.

"Isn't Johnny Waco the cutest guy you've ever seen?" Frankie whispered to Emily.

"Nobody's cute when they've just sucked the blood out of an innocent victim," Emily said with a shiver.

"But he bit her so they can spend all eternity together," Frankie protested. "Now Belinda Blythe will be a vampire, too. That's true love."

"That's not true love," said Emily. "That's disgusting."

Billy Lopez and Spike Piranna walked over to the group of people waiting to choose their lunch from a buffet table.

"That movie blood's cool," said Spike, his eyes glittering. "It sure looks real."

"It does," said Billy, whose father created special effects for movies, "even though it's just made out of corn syrup and food coloring."

The five members of the Canal Street Club heaped their plates with hamburgers, French fries, and brownies.

Spike, Billy, Frankie, and Emily had first formed the club two years earlier when Tulu was in kindergarten and the rest of the kids were in third grade at Washington Elementary school. They had been holding weekly meetings in Spike's grandparents' attic ever since.

Last spring, the Canal Street kids had tied with Bunny Bigalow and Violetta Epstein for first place in the school fair. The prize was that they were allowed to be extras in this Johnny Waco movie, *Crypt Riders in the Night.*

Carefully holding their plates and sodas, the kids walked over to the porch of the sheriff's office to eat their lunch. Frankie tossed her blond hair dramatically and smoothed the skirt of her long gingham dress. Then she sat down on the steps that faced the dusty street.

"I can't believe this is happening," Frankie said. "It's a dream come true." Her eyes followed Johnny Waco as he walked slowly across the movie set designed to look like a small western town.

"All this waiting gets boring after a while," Billy said. He had been on lots of sets while movies were being made.

"I can't imagine *ever* getting bored," Frankie answered, enthralled by all the scenes she'd been in. "It took a lot of practice for me to capture the drama of walking across a school yard the way I did in that last shot."

Billy looked sideways at his friend. "Practice?" he asked. "How dramatic can walking across a school yard be?"

Just as he finished his question, Bunny Bigalow and Violetta Epstein sauntered toward the group.

Bunny and Violetta were the two most stuck-up girls in school. And nobody in the Canal Street Club got along with them.

"This pasta primavera is simply *superb*," said Bunny as she daintily pressed a napkin to her lips.

"I prefer the salad," Violetta answered in her phony adult voice. "Hamburgers and French fries are too greasy and fattening. An actress has to keep a slim figure. Besides," she added, "the pasta has garlic in it. And I hate garlic."

Frankie glanced down at her heaping plate and wondered if she should only eat one helping of French fries instead of two.

Violetta looked at Spike and smiled. "Hi, Spike," she said, batting her eyelashes as she spoke.

Momentarily stunned by the friendliness of Violetta's greeting, nobody said a word. Instead, they just stared at their two longtime enemies as they walked on down the street toward the general store.

What on earth was *that* all about? Spike thought, confused at being treated so nicely by Violetta Epstein, a girl who had spent the last four years being nasty to him. Frankie looked at Spike and giggled. "I don't believe it," she said. "I just don't believe it. Violetta Epstein has a crush on you."

Spike's expression looked like he had just bitten into a lemon. "Gimme a break," he said.

"It's true," Emily snickered. "Didn't you see the

way she fluttered her stubby lashes at you? Girls can tell about those things."

Spike put his finger in his open mouth and made a gagging sound. "Who does Violetta think she's kidding?" he asked. "She's got to be up to no good if she's being nice to me," he said.

"They're not kidding *us*, that's for sure," Frankie said. "Those two never even thanked us for being here. It's only because they ruined our toe show at the school fair that the contest was declared a tie. Believe me, displaying Emily's father's toe in a matchbox was a much better booth than just selling cupcakes and brownies. If Bunny and Violetta hadn't made such a mess of our toe show, we would have earned the most money and been the only winners of the Grand Prize. And they wouldn't be in this movie at all."

"That's the truth," said Spike, still puzzled by the friendly expression in Violetta's blue eyes.

"Well, we're stuck with them and we might as well make the best of it," Emily said in her most positive voice. "The good part is we don't have to talk to them. All we have to do is be in the same movie with them."

"I just hope they're not in more scenes than we are," Frankie said, swinging her long blond hair out of her face with a practiced toss of her head. "This is my movie debut, and I'll just *die* if they have more time on screen than we do."

Billy looked at Frankie and shook his head. "We're just extras," he said matter-of-factly. "By the end of the movie, we'll probably all end up on the cutting-room floor."

Frankie's eyes opened wide. "Never!" she exclaimed.

"You mean they're going to cut us up?" Tulu asked fearfully.

Emily patted Frankie's little sister on her shoulder. "Not the blood kind of cut," she said. Then she explained that what Billy meant was that sometimes in movies the director decides not to use some of the scenes.

"You mean we can do all this working and waiting and then not be in the movie when they show it?" Tulu asked.

"It happens all the time," Billy said with a shrug.

"Well it better not happen to me," Frankie said. She had been dreaming of being a movie star since the day she got Miss Piggy's autograph in a shopping mall. "I'm counting on this movie to launch my acting career."

"I'm counting on the money I earn in this movie to buy Noah Benchley's deluxe ant farm," said Billy. "He's got an awesome queen ant."

"And I'm counting on this movie to learn more about vampires," Spike said, his eyes glittering with excitement. "They might even have actual vampires on the set as expert advisers."

Emily scrunched up her face. "No way," she said with a wave of her hand. "There's no such thing as a vampire."

"Grandma says there is," Spike said with certainty. "She says she met one in the old country."

All the kids knew Spike's grandmother because he lived with his grandparents. Grandma Piranna was born in Transylvania, the home of the original Count Dracula. She was, she claimed, part gypsy. Not only did she know how to read palms and tell fortunes from tea leaves, she knew how to identify vampires and werewolves.

Emily cocked her head. "Even if there were vampires," she said skeptically, "they wouldn't be out in broad daylight."

"Well," Spike said. "Grandma says it's all Hollywood nonsense that vampires can't be out in the daytime. They just prefer the night, that's all."

Their conversation was suddenly interrupted by Clyde Perkins. Clap-clap! Clap-clap-clap! "Okay, everyone, quiet on the set!" he called out.

The Canal Street kids walked over to the Red Dirt Saloon and sat quietly on a bench as they watched a gunfight being filmed between Johnny Waco and the town sheriff.

Several of Johnny's vampire cowboy friends stood across the street, prepared to cheer him on as he faced the sheriff. They were dressed in western clothes. Two of the men had thick hair on their

hands and a pink tinge to their eyes.

"Look at their hands and eyes," said Tulu.

"Sure signs they're vampires," whispered Spike.

Belinda Blythe, looking beautiful in a blue-flowered calico dress, stood to one side.

"Roll cameras!" called the director.

In the background, Johnny's blood-sucking friends leaned closer, their eyes glinting crimson in the noonday sun. Pursing her ruby red lips, Belinda Blythe blew Johnny a kiss.

Johnny winked at her and smiled, adjusting his legs into gunfight position before he bravely turned to face the sheriff.

"There's not enough room in this town for the two of us," growled the sheriff.

"That's what I'm thinking!" cried Johnny Waco, standing in the middle of the dusty street.

Without warning, the sheriff drew his gun and aimed it at Johnny.

Bang! Bang! Bang!

"Aaargh!" cried Johnny Waco, throwing his hand over his heart and breaking the bag of stage blood that had been tucked into his pocket before the scene began.

"No, Johnnyyyy Nooooo!" cried Belinda, her canine teeth shining brightly behind her blood-red lips.

Shaking his head disdainfully, the sheriff took one final look at his enemy and walked away.

Blood spurted from between Johnny's fingers as an expression of rage spread over his face. From across the street, Belinda ran to Johnny's side.

"Are you all right?" she asked, kneeling down in the dust to help her long-toothed lover.

Johnny coughed fitfully. Then with a soft laugh, he said, "Oh, Belinda, don't you cry for me. Now that you're one of us, you ought to know that vampires don't die from regular bullets. It takes silver bullets to bring us down."

"Cut!" called Sylvia Kirk, the director.

"*Powerful* scene," said Frankie, wiping away a tear. "*Brilliant* acting."

Tulu shuddered. "Do you think Belinda Blythe is a real vampire?" she asked, admiring the beautiful red-eyed woman.

"Of course not," said Billy. "She's made up to look like one. She's wearing red contact lenses."

"Besides, not all vampires look like that," said Spike. "Unless you know the signs, you can't tell a vampire from an ordinary person."

Frankie shivered. "Then how do we know who's a vampire and who isn't?" she asked.

"Besides hair on their hands, and red eyes, they usually have pale skin and red lips, too."

"Just like Violetta Epstein," Tulu said.

"Yeah," Spike said. "You should also look for those long side teeth."

"The canines," said Billy.

Spike nodded. "Yeah, right, long canines. And vampires also have cold skin and sometimes their eyebrows meet over the nose."

"Like Violetta," Tulu repeated.

"Right," Spike agreed. "But lots of people have things like that, so it's hard to tell. Grandma says that some real-life vampires have pointy ears and long fingernails."

"Spooky," Billy said, casually checking out the ears of his friends.

"But the way you can really tell," Spike continued, "is that vampires have no reflection in the mirror."

Just then, the assistant director came up to the group of kids and smiled.

"Okay," Clyde Perkins said, sitting down next to them. "We're almost ready for the body in the coffin scene."

"Is the body Johnny Waco?" Frankie asked hopefully.

Spike rolled his eyes. She's got lots of nerve teasing me about Violetta, he thought, when she's got such a thing for that vampire cowboy.

Clyde nodded. "Yes, dear, the body is Johnny Waco," he said, smiling indulgently and patting Frankie on her head. "So get on over to the undertaker's with your friends here. We're about ready to start."

Bunny and Violetta were waiting when the

Canal Street kids arrived at the undertaker's set. Instead of ignoring them, the two girls immediately scurried over to the group.

"Guess what!" Violetta simpered, excitement spilling out of her voice. "Bunny and I get big parts in this scene!"

Hypnotized by Violetta's red lips and long canine teeth, Tulu shuddered. What if Spike's grandmother was right?

CHAPTER TWO

The Canal Street kids stood on the set of the undertaker's building. Wooden coffins were stacked like building blocks next to an open window. In the center of the room, Johnny Waco lay in his coffin as he waited for the director's signal.

Clap-clap!

The kids turned to Clyde Perkins. "All right, people!" he said. "This is the scene where Johnny turns into a bat."

"Why would he want to do that?" asked Tulu.

Violetta pursed her lips. "All vampires can turn into bats at night. Didn't you know that?" she asked.

"But how will they make him into a bat?" Tulu persisted.

Violetta opened her mouth, but no words came out. Unable to answer the question, she looked away.

Billy smiled at Tulu. "It will probably be done with computer morphing," he explained. "My dad knows how to do that."

"Right you are," confirmed Clyde. "Now

remember," he said in his organized voice as he looked at the Canal Street kids. "You've sneaked into the undertaker's basement to look at the body. You think you're alone. But then Violetta and Bunny appear. When they stand up, you turn and hurry back up the stairs."

After the kids finished practicing their moves, the assistant director called for quiet on the set so filming could begin.

The Canal Street kids finished their scene in three takes. Then they sat on the stairs and watched the next scene being filmed.

"Would you look at those two!" Frankie hissed as Bunny and Violetta practiced their special scene, when they peeked out from behind a coffin to inspect Johnny's body. "They overact and they walk like klutzes!"

"Quiet on the set!" yelled Sylvia Kirk, the director, looking right at Frankie. "Cameras are ready to roll!"

Frankie blushed as the camera began to shoot the scene of Bunny and Violetta and Johnny Waco as he rose from the coffin.

When the filming was finished, Sylvia Kirk walked over to the cameraman to discuss final plans for the next shot. As she spoke, another camera was positioned on the back of the truck in order to shoot Johnny Waco as he rode into town.

Suddenly, Sylvia nodded and turned to Clyde

Perkins. "I need kids for this scene, after all. Get me three of those rug rats," she said in a curt voice. "Two girls and a boy."

Clyde walked over and looked at the assembled children. "I need three of you for a scene. Two girls and a boy." Before he finished the sentence, Frankie shot her hand in the air and waved it frantically.

He laughed. "All right, you," he said to Frankie.

Tossing her long blond hair, Frankie smiled and stepped past Bunny and Violetta.

Reacting like she had been shot from a cannon, Violetta jumped out of the crowd. "Oh, Mr. Perkins!" She called out in a voice dripping with sugar. "Mr. Perkins!"

The assistant director looked at Violetta.

"I can do it. I've been taking acting lessons for three months," she said. "Let me do it . . . *Please* . . ."

"You're on," he said.

Violetta hesitated, then she pointed to Spike. "He's an excellent actor," she said.

Mr. Perkins looked at Violetta. "If you say so, kid," he said.

Frankie, Violetta, and Spike walked with the assistant director toward the middle of the street.

"Let's see some hustle there," the director called out. "You're not being paid to stand around."

"I thought we *were* being paid to stand around," Tulu piped up as Violetta, Spike, and Frankie hurried to meet the director.

"Tell them what to do, Perkins, while I finish up here," said Sylvia Kirk.

"Right!" Clyde Perkins said with an efficient nod of his head. Then he turned to Violetta, Spike, and Frankie.

"Okay, kids. When Johnny looks at you, you're supposed to be afraid. Show me how you look when you're frightened."

Without a sound, Violetta demonstrated an expression of terror.

"Wonderful," said Perkins. "And you?" he said to Spike.

Spike thought of the time he almost stepped on a rattlesnake.

"Good," said Perkins. "And you?"

Filled with excitement, Frankie took a dramatic breath, then cried out in terror. Suddenly moving her hand to her mouth, she opened her eyes wide, then turned her gaze upward as she slumped into a swoon.

Mr. Perkins frowned. "That's a bit much," he said. "Can you tone it down a little?"

Frankie nodded nervously and repeated her wide-eyed gesture of fear, this time clutching at her throat and shivering as if she were standing stark naked in the middle of an Arctic winter.

Mr. Perkins sighed. "Better," he said. "But try it without the shiver next time."

"Right," said Frankie.

"Okay, kids," said Sylvia Kirk. "I want to get this in one shot, so listen up. Johnny rides into town fast. You're crossing the street just as he turns the corner. He almost runs over you. You scream and scramble out of the way as fast as you can. Got it?"

"Cool," said Spike.

Frankie swallowed apprehensively.

Violetta batted her eyelashes at Spike. "You're so brave."

Sylvia Kirk sighed impatiently. "Not to worry. This is going to be filmed in front of a blue screen."

"What's that?" asked Frankie.

Clyde Perkins explained that using a blue screen was a safe way to film a dangerous scene in a movie. A blue background doesn't show up on film, so anything—from mountains to a cattle stampede—can be added later by substituting it for the blue screen. "In this case," he said, "after we finish filming Johnny galloping around the corner, we'll add it to the scene where you're scrambling out of the way. We don't want you to risk being trampled by a horse."

"And we don't want to risk being sued for ten million dollars, either," added Sylvia Kirk with a nasty smile.

After positioning the three kids in the street, the director looked at them and said, "We'll rehearse once, then shoot." She jerked her head at the assistant director, winding him up once again.

"Okay," said Clyde, "when you hear the director yell 'action,' start walking across the street. Then, when you get to the line drawn in the dirt near the middle of the street, look to your right and register terror. Imagine a horse is bearing down on you. You'll be trampled if you don't get out of the way. You scream, then run for the sidewalk . . ." he paused. "Ready?"

The children nodded.

"Ready. Roll sound . . . roll cameras . . . and *action!*"

The three kids began to walk across the dirt street. The moment she reached the mark, Frankie jerked her head to the right and stared into the blue nothingness with terror. Gasping, she threw her arms up and successfully blocked Violetta's face from the camera with her hand. Then, with a scream, she scrambled out of the way of the imaginary hooves.

Seizing her opportunity, Violetta threw her arms around Spike. Burying her face in his shoulder, she shrieked, "Save me!"

As she tried to cling tighter to him, Spike looked stunned.

Caught in the middle of her scream, Frankie choked, sputtered and then moved into a coughing fit. At the same time, Spike broke Violetta's grip so he could run across the street to escape the imaginary horse's hooves—and Violetta.

"Cut!" yelled the director. Then she turned to Frankie. "What was *that?*" she asked sarcastically.

Still coughing, Frankie choked, "I'm sorry. I'll do better next time."

"Forget it. There *is* no next time. We're behind schedule and we have to go with what we've got."

After that scene Ms. Blight, the teacher-social worker, informed the director that the children had already been on the set for eight hours. They weren't allowed to stay any longer.

So the Canal Street kids, along with Bunny and Violetta, headed for the general store. Their parents would be waiting in the parking lot behind the set to drive them home.

As they walked into the fake building, the group passed a large mirror mounted in a fancy gold frame.

We look just like pioneer kids, Spike thought as he caught a glimpse of himself in the mirror wearing dusty boots, faded overalls, and a worn plaid shirt. It took him a minute to realize that although Violetta Epstein was standing in front of him, there was no reflection of her in the mirror.

Holy cow! Spike thought. He closed his eyes and shook his head. But when he opened his eyes and looked again, nothing had changed. He could see himself clearly in the mirror. Violetta was standing in front of him. But there was no reflection of her. None at all.

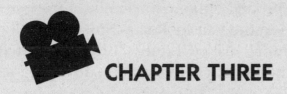

CHAPTER THREE

With his heart beating in his throat, Spike looked around the general store. Breathless, he spotted his friends and hurried over to them.

"You're not going to believe this," he croaked, "but I promise it's true."

"What?" asked Tulu.

"What?" asked the others.

"Violetta's a vampire!" Spike said. "A real vampire. And I've got proof!"

"No way!" declared Emily.

At that moment, Ms. Blight approached the group.

"Later!" whispered Spike.

"Billy," said Ms. Blight cheerfully, "your dad's outside waiting for you in the car."

"Thank you," Billy said politely, then turned to Frankie, Emily, Tulu, and Spike. "Let's go," he said.

In the backseat of the car Billy leaned close to Spike. "Do you really think Violetta's a vampire?" he asked.

"Yep," Spike said.

"No way," declared Emily with certainty.

"I've got proof," Spike whispered.

Every kid in the van looked at Spike.

"What proof?" asked Emily. "I don't care what your grandmother says, there's no such thing as a vampire."

Spike hesitated, then jerked his head toward Mr. Lopez. "We can't talk about it here," he said in an excited whisper.

Everyone nodded.

"Then as president of the Canal Street Club," Frankie said, "I'm calling an emergency meeting for right after dinner." She looked at Spike with her squinty-eyed, serious-business expression. "Your evidence better be good," she said. "Because I don't call an emergency meeting unless it's really important."

Spike looked at her and snorted. "Don't worry," he said. "You won't be disappointed."

It was almost seven o'clock when the kids finished dinner and arrived at Spike's house.

As soon as they had climbed into the attic, Frankie said, "Okay, everyone. Settle down and be quiet. We have serious business to take care of."

The kids grabbed their pillows and sat down in a circle.

"All right," said Frankie in her presidential voice. "This official emergency meeting of the Canal Street Club will now come to order."

As soon as she finished the sentence, Spike's hand shot up.

"Okay, Spike." said Frankie. "Tell us about your proof that Violetta's a vampire."

"Well," said Spike, "you know that mirror in the general store?"

Everyone nodded.

"I stood in front of that mirror right next to Violetta. And . . ." he paused dramatically, "she didn't have a reflection."

Tulu's mouth dropped open. Frankie's eyes widened. Emily looked skeptical. "Wait a minute!" she said. The kids looked at her expectantly. "Aren't we missing something here? The fact is vampires aren't real. They're only make-believe monsters invented by some writer a hundred years ago."

"Not according to Grandma Piranna," said Spike stubbornly.

"Not according to *Bloodsucker Tales*, either," said Billy.

Emily threw up her hands. "Listen, Billy," she said. "Just because *Bloodsucker Tales* is your favorite comic book doesn't mean it tells the truth."

"Wait a minute!" said Spike. "I told everything! You guys are missing the point here." He held up his right hand, his palm facing toward his friends. "It happened. I swear it happened. I stood in front of a real mirror. I had a reflection and Violetta didn't."

"Maybe she *is* a vampire," said Billy.

"Just thinking of Violetta gives me the creeps," Tulu said.

"Gives *you* the creeps," said Spike. "What about me? It makes me wonder why she's being so nice to me all of a sudden."

"We already told you . . . she's got a crush on you," said Emily.

"I don't know," Frankie said carefully. "What if it's more than a crush? What if she grabbed you in that horse-trampling scene because she wanted to bite you?" She paused and thought a moment. "What if it's like Johnny Waco turning Belinda Blythe into a vampire so he could spend all eternity with her?"

"All eternity?" Spike said. "I couldn't spend more than five minutes with Violetta."

"I'm serious, Spike," said Frankie. "If we don't do something about it, you could be sprouting fangs by your next birthday."

Suddenly the room turned silent. Nobody moved. Nobody said a word.

Frankie took a deep breath, then continued. "Well," she said finally. "We definitely need a plan."

Just then, Grandma Piranna called up the stairs. "If you kids are hungry, I've got some leftovers for you in the kitchen."

"Great!" said Billy.

"Maybe Grandma will have some ideas," Spike said.

"What smells so good?" Frankie asked when they walked into the kitchen.

Grandma Piranna smiled, turning her face into a friendly mass of wrinkles. "Garlic bread," she said. "One of my specialties. Would you like a piece?"

"Sure!" said Frankie, who was always hungry.

"And help yourself to some fruit," Grandma Piranna said as she set a platter of sliced apples and watermelon on the table.

"We've been wondering," Billy said. "We're in this vampire movie, and if there were actually such a thing as a real vampire, what could you do to keep it away?"

As she put the long loaf of fragrant French bread on the cutting board, sliced it, and handed out thick pieces, Grandma Piranna said, "First of all, there are no 'ifs' about it. Vampires have always been with us. They are as real as you and me. And second, you're eating the best antivampire medicine there is."

Tulu looked at her friends. Then she looked around the room. Puzzled, she asked, "Garlic bread?"

Grandma Piranna reached into a bowl on the counter and held up a clove of garlic. "This is it," she said. "Garlic not only keeps you healthy, it also keeps vampires away."

"I remember that. I read about it in *Bloodsucker Tales*," said Billy. "Vampires hate the smell. So if you wear it, they won't touch you."

"That's right, Billy," said Grandma Piranna.

After thanking her, the five Canal Street Club members returned to the attic.

"So garlic it is," said Frankie. "That's our protection. Starting tomorrow, we all wear it." She paused. "And that goes for you, too, Emily. We'd never forgive ourselves if Violetta bit you because you weren't wearing your garlic for protection."

Emily rolled her eyes. "Okay, okay," she said. "Even though I think it's stupid, I'll go along with the plan."

"This emergency meeting of the Canal Street Club is now officially adjourned," said Frankie.

The kids dropped their pillows and gathered in a circle. Extending their arms into the center, they gripped each other's hands, pumping their arms up and down three times. "Canal Street Forever!" they chanted. "Forever and ever!" Then they went downstairs.

Outside, Tulu and Frankie turned toward home, while Emily and Billy continued to the end of the block.

The twilight sun cast long shadows on the wide sidewalk that divided the houses lining each side of Canal Street. Emily and Billy carried their skateboards, munching their garlic bread as they walked.

In the dim glow of dusk, the bushes looked dark and foreboding. The evening breeze created changing patterns of light and shadow from constantly moving tree branches, and the eerie call of crickets warned it soon would be dark.

Emily glanced behind her at the shadows that followed her and Billy.

"It's creepy out here," said Billy.

"Speaking of creepy," said Emily, "let's go see what Violetta the so-called vampire's up to."

"I have to be home by dark," Billy said.

"It's not dark yet," said Emily, glancing at the pearl-gray sky. "It's only twilight. We have time."

Violetta Epstein lived three blocks away on Austin Avenue.

"Okay," Billy said. "But we have to hurry."

Before they started walking, Emily tugged at Billy's sleeve. "Billy?" she said thoughtfully. "Something's bugging me . . . something about Violetta, but I can't remember what it is."

"I hate when that happens," said Billy. "It's like having a burp that won't come up."

Emily smiled. "Well, I hope it comes up soon. It's driving me nuts."

Carefully, Billy and Emily approached Violetta's house, staying in the shadows whenever possible. When they reached the black picket fence that outlined Violetta's front yard, they stopped.

"Would you look at that?" Emily whispered, pointing to Mr. Epstein's withered cactus garden. "What a mess," she added, shaking her head.

Mr. Epstein's hobbies were famous. He chose a new one almost every year. His interest in cacti three years ago had been replaced by fossils. After he had a pile of old rocks spilling off of his work desk in the basement, he decided to change to a hobby that didn't use so much space. That's when he decided to take up needlepoint.

The front porch of Violetta's house had been built by Mr. Epstein during his woodworking period. At one end of the porch, an old-fashioned wooden swing was suspended from the rafters by brass chains. On the swing, Violetta's entire doll collection sat nestled on the elegant needlepoint pillows Mr. Epstein had designed.

"Would you get a look at all those dolls," Emily said scornfully.

"Hard to believe," Billy said, shaking his head as his eyes scanned past the row of dolls. Each one was dressed in a different outfit: a doctor, a secretary, a bride, even a surfer. Every doll had her own "date," too. *Really* hard to believe."

"Shhh," whispered Emily. "There's her room." She pointed to the lighted window over the front porch.

Billy glanced up just in time to see Violetta.

"Duck!" he hissed.

Crouching behind the fence, Billy and Emily watched as Violetta raised her arms, stretching them wide above her head.

"Weird," Billy said.

Before he could even finish his sentence, a strange whirring sound filled the air, then a dark cloud swooped from the back of Violetta's house and flew right toward Emily and Billy.

"What's that?" Emily gasped.

The vibrating, whirring shadow headed straight toward them. Holding their skateboards over their heads for protection, Emily and Billy crouched low on the sidewalk as the noisy mass of moving shadows swooped past.

"Bats," said Billy, shaking his head in wonder. "That was actually a flock of bats."

For a long moment, Emily didn't say a word. Then she looked back at Violetta's window. Violetta Epstein had disappeared.

Emily took a deep breath. "Vampires turn into bats at night."

Billy nodded. "That's what *Bloodsucker Tales* says."

Emily paused. "I got it," she said with a shudder. "I remembered what I was trying to remember." Her voice was grim.

"Yeah?"

"Violetta hates garlic. She can't stand the stuff."

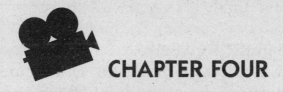

CHAPTER FOUR

"What do you mean that 'Violetta has bats in her belfry?'" Tulu said the next morning on the movie lot.

Billy glanced around the movie set, making certain that nobody except the Canal Street kids were nearby. "I mean," he said, "that a flock of bats flew out from behind Violetta's house. We saw them with our·own eyes."

"Cool . . ." said Spike.

Wide-eyed, Tulu stood silently by Spike's side.

"Honest," Emily said, crossing her heart and kissing her elbow. "There were lots of them, too," said Emily.

"Not only that," Billy continued in a hoarse whisper. "When the bats came out, Violetta disappeared from the window."

"It's true," said Emily, her copper-colored curls bouncing back and forth like she was wearing a scouring pad on her head. "Vampires turn into bats. Violetta disappeared when the bats appeared. You can put two and two together."

"Four!" said Tulu.

"Right," said Emily. "I've got all the proof I needed."

"That's the truth," said Spike.

Emily held up a pouch filled with garlic puree that hung suspended from her sash. "It's a good thing we came well-prepared," she said, squeezing the pouch and causing a stream of garlic juice to drip onto her dress. "You know how Violetta hates garlic."

Spike popped another clove of garlic into his mouth and munched it slowly. He had been eating them like Lifesavers since he left the house that morning.

"Yeah . . ." Billy said, stepping away from Spike to avoid his reeking breath. "Violetta's the real thing, all right—a vampire who can turn herself into a bat at night." He pulled out his herb bottle and sprinkled garlic powder in his hands. Then he put some in the cuffs of his pants and poured a little more into his shirt pocket for additional protection.

A chill shimmied up Tulu's back as she reached over and took Spike's hand in hers. With her other hand, she touched the necklace of five garlic cloves she had strung on silver thread the night before. Frankie wore one, too.

The five kids turned to look at Violetta who stood on the porch in front of the sheriff's office. She and Bunny were caught up in a lively conversation with Mr. Perkins.

"Mr. Perkins better be careful or she might turn him into a vampire, too," said Tulu. "Maybe we should warn him."

Billy shook his head. "You know how grown-ups are. We'd go to all the trouble of telling him and he wouldn't believe us," he said. "We're the only ones who know the real truth."

Nodding vigorously, Spike said, "Besides, if we want grown-ups to believe us, we'd have to catch her in the act. Nab her red-handed in front of other people."

"You should have turned her in yesterday when she tried to bite your neck while we were filming," said Frankie.

Spike's face paled. "I can't believe she almost got me in broad daylight," he said.

"Vampires will do anything if they're desperate enough," Billy said. "In an emergency, they'll eat anything. I read about a vampire who couldn't find any humans on this desert island, and he got so hungry he attacked a rat."

"Grandma says they'll suck the blood from any animal if things get bad enough," said Spike, glancing at Clementine, Johnny Waco's horse, as she munched oats from a bucket next to where Bunny and Violetta stood with Mr. Perkins.

"What are we going to do about this?" Tulu asked.

"The best thing we can do," said Emily, "is to make sure nobody is left alone with Violetta." She looked over at Bunny and Violetta. "And I mean nobody . . . beginning right now," she added with fierce determination.

"You're right," said Frankie. Standing up straighter, she squared her shoulders and walked over to where Bunny, Violetta, and Mr. Perkins stood.

Mr. Perkins greeted Frankie with a smile, then a puzzled expression came over his face. "What's that smell?" he asked.

From across the dusty street, Sylvia Kirk called out, "Perkins! Where the heck are you! We're ready to shoot *now!*"

Clyde Perkins stiffened. Then, as if a make-up person had just pasted a smile on his face, he grinned at Sylvia and raised his hands into dance position. Clap-clap! Clap-clap! "All right, people! Ready in the general store!"

One by one the Canal Street kids followed Mr. Perkins, Violetta, and Bunny to the general store. They stood on the set and listened to the assistant director tell the extras to pretend they were shopping. Then, when Johnny Waco walked through the room, they should look at him in fear. "Remember," he said to Violetta. "You're the only person in the store who isn't worried about being turned into a vampire. You're an innocent child."

"Hah!" Frankie muttered to Emily. "That's what he thinks."

"You're the only one who's not scared," the assistant director continued. "Johnny will stop next to you to look at a pair of spurs in the display case. Do it just like we practiced," he said.

Violetta nodded as the director said, "Quiet on the set . . . roll sound . . . roll camera . . . and . . . *action!*"

Everyone in the store looked busy for a moment, then Johnny Waco entered the door. The people looked up, expressions of fear and surprise on their faces. As the group backed away from the vampire cowboy, only Violetta, absorbed in examining the bolts of fabric, failed to notice him. As she held up a piece of blue-and-yellow calico, Johnny strode over to her and patted her on the head. Then Violetta turned and, with a broad smile that revealed her long side teeth, reached for his hand.

"No!" gasped Tulu, running over to her sister's hero to save him from Violetta the vampire. "No, Johnny! Don't let her touch you!"

"Cut!" yelled the director, her face red with fury.

"What's that smell?" Johnny asked, totally confused.

"You've ruined my scene, Tulu Stevens!" Violetta shrieked. "You've ruined my big moment!"

"*Your* big moment?" Sylvia Kirk said in disbelief as she stalked over to the group.

"What's that smell?" Johnny asked again. But nobody listened.

Suddenly Bunny Bigalow ran across the set to

her friend's side. Glaring hard at Tulu, she said, "How could you do that?"

Tears welled in Tulu's eyes. "I . . ." she sobbed. "I only wanted—"

Furious, Frankie, Spike, Billy, and Emily ran to Tulu's side.

"You can't do that to my little sister!" Frankie yelled at Bunny. "You can't make her cry like that!"

Bunny sneered. "Looks like I already did."

"Mr. Perkins!" Violetta wailed as she stomped her foot. "They've ruined my best scene! Make them go home!" Angry tears rolled down her face as she stomped her feet over and over again. "Make them go home now!"

"Make *us* go home," Billy said.

"Us?" said Spike.

"Why don't *you* go home?" demanded Emily. "You're the one who's dangerous."

Stunned beyond words, Clyde Perkins stood silent as he watched the chaotic scene unfold before him. Shocked beyond speech, Sylvia Kirk stood mute with amazement.

"What is that *smell?*" Johnny asked again.

"Me go home?" shrieked Violetta, flailing her arms and stomping her feet again and again and again.

"You!" snarled Frankie.

Ms. Blight scurried over to the set. "What's going on here?" she asked in her school-teacher-welfare-worker voice.

"It appears," said Sylvia Kirk, slowly regaining her power of speech, "that this brat here is having a fit." With a trembling hand, Sylvia pointed at Violetta. "I'm a director, not a baby-sitter. And I'll shoot that scene with a *donkey* before I'll use these kids again today. Get them out of here."

Stiffening her shoulders, Ms. Blight turned to the kids. "Quickly now, children," she said. "Quickly! We'll have to be leaving right this second."

"I better go call my mother and ask her to pick up Violetta and me early," Bunny said.

"I need to call, too," said Emily. "Where's the phone?"

"Over there," Ms. Blight said, pointing toward the office. "Hurry now, children," she said. "Hurry up."

As Bunny and Violetta ran toward the door, the Canal Street Club members followed on their heels. They all ran to the back of the general store and through the opening into the adjoining room.

"We get to use the phone first!" Violetta shrieked.

"We're first in line!" said Bunny. "Wait your turn!"

Violetta bolted through the door with Bunny right behind her.

"Not so fast," yelled Frankie, shoving her foot in the door. "We have just as much right to the phone as you do!"

Grabbing the knob, Spike held the door open for

Emily, Frankie, Tulu, and Billy, then stepped inside and slammed the door behind him.

Suddenly the entire group found itself trapped in total darkness.

"Where's the light?" Bunny cried out.

Frankie gasped. "Violetta Epstein, you turn on the light right this instant! If you think you're going to get away with this, you're crazy!"

"Get away with what?" Violetta asked.

"Don't play innocent with us!" Billy said.

"That's right," said Tulu. "Don't play innocent with us!"

"Just turn on the light right now!" Spike said.

"I can't see anything. How do you expect me to turn on the light?" Violetta said as her elbow bumped into a stack of boxes.

"Let's get out of here!" cried Frankie.

"Where's the door?" said Emily.

"Yuck! What's that disgusting smell?" asked Violetta. Groping for the door, she whined, "The smell's making me sick. I have to get out of here." Just then she bumped into Tulu.

"Don't touch me!" Tulu screamed as she stumbled away from Violetta and fell against Spike.

Thrown off balance, Spike stepped sideways and caught his heel in the hem of Violetta's dress.

Riiip!

"Who stepped on my dress!" Violetta wailed. "Who tore my beautiful movie dress?'

Moving backwards, Bunny knocked over a wet mop that had been placed against the wall to dry.

CRASH! BAM!

"Eeeeekkk!" Tulu yelled as the slimy strings of the mop brushed past her face. "I'm being attacked by Violetta!"

"What!" Billy said, trying to find Tulu and avoid Violetta. As he stepped forward, arms extended, he toppled a can from one of the shelves. Splash . . . plop . . .

Something sticky and gooey splattered everywhere drop by drop by messy drop.

Unable to bear it another moment, Violetta opened her mouth and howled at the top of her lungs.

"HHEEELP!" Her voice traveled past the closed door and into the crowded room of the general store. "HHHEEEEELLP MEEE!"

After a few breathless moments, the door opened wide.

"What the . . ." Johnny Waco said as he reached inside the door and switched on the light.

The kids hadn't walked into an office at all. Instead, Violetta Epstein had led them right into a cluttered storage closet.

"More to the point," continued Johnny Waco, "What *is* that foul smell?"

Sylvia Kirk pushed her way into the open doorway. Stunned, she stared at the children as the

pungent odor of garlic assaulted her senses. "I'm *trying* to make a movie here." She glared at Perkins. "I want this mess cleaned up pronto! As for you," she said, turning back to the children, "Get out of your costumes and off of my set this minute. Out! You're through, finished! Finito!"

"For the day?" asked Violetta in her sweetest voice as she stepped out of the closet. Her torn dress was covered with fake blood, and gray, slimy strings from the mop hung off the side of her head.

"You figure it out," said the director.

CHAPTER FIVE

The Canal Street kids stood quietly in the parking lot. Beside them, Clementine munched contentedly on her oats while three actors rehearsed a scene in the corner.

"My career is ruined!" Frankie moaned softly. "They've taken my hopes, my dreams, my costume." She paused a moment, wiping the tears from her cheek with the back of her hand. "I didn't even get Johnny Waco's autograph. The only thing I got for my effort is fake blood all over my arm."

"Ms. Blight said it would wash off when we take a bath," Emily said, rubbing her hand over the patch of blood that covered her cheek.

Billy reached up and felt his stiff, sticky hair as Tulu inspected her blood-stained hand. Then she leaned over and patted her sister on the arm. "Don't worry, Frankie," she said. "Your career isn't over. You'll just have to get discovered a little later, that's all."

"Tulu's right," Billy said.

"Besides," added Spike, "we've already been in lots of scenes."

Frankie squinted her eyes. "Scenes aren't the problem. Violetta is," she said. "Something has to be done about her."

Just then, Bunny and Violetta walked out the back door. Her eyes red from crying and her hand smeared with fake blood, Violetta looked at the club members and stamped her foot.

"It's all your fault," she said. "You've ruined my chance to be in a movie!"

"Ruined it!" said Bunny, nodding her head.

"What did you expect us to do?" Billy asked. "Just stand around and do nothing while you turned everyone into a vampire?"

Violetta stared at him, her red eyes blazing.

"Wh-what are you talking about?" Violetta asked, scrunching up her face.

"Bunny darling!" cried Mrs. Bigalow as she stepped out of her car. "Violetta! Come along, dears. I have to stop by the market on the way home."

Violetta shot Frankie a nasty look. "Coming, Mrs. Bigalow!" she said sweetly.

As they drove out of the parking lot, Bunny and Violetta sat huddled in the backseat. Just as they passed the Canal Street kids, Violetta rolled down the window with her bloody hand and hollered, "I'll get even with you for this! Just you wait and see! You'll all be . . ." Her last word, "S-O-R-R-Y-Y-Y!"

seemed to echo off the walls of the set and hang in the air as the car sped away.

Just then, Emily's father drove into the parking area. Sitting proudly behind the wheel of his brand-new bright red luxury van, he was thrilled to have the opportunity to show off his car on an actual movie lot. Eager to announce his new status to the world, his license plate read DR. SYKE, advertising the fact that he had recently earned his Ph.D. in psychology.

"Hey, kids!" Dr. Anderson said as he bounded out of his car. Squinting, he reached in his pocket and pulled out a handkerchief, then briskly removed a small spot of dust on the hood.

Smiling, he turned and took a good look at the kids. His eyes popped out when he saw that they were covered with blood.

"What happened!" he cried, running to Emily.

"We're okay," Emily said. "It's the fake stuff."

"Oh," he said with a chuckle. "I see. Stage blood. That stuff sure looks real." He paused, then sniffed the air. "But it really stinks."

Emily took a deep breath. "Yep," she said.

Dr. Anderson smiled his psychologist smile. "This has been quite an experience for you kids, hasn't it?"

You don't know the half of it, thought Spike.

That evening, the Canal Street kids met for a special dinner conference in the attic.

"The meeting will officially come to order," said

Frankie. Without waiting for comments from anyone else, she said, "The first order of business is to figure out what to do about Violetta."

"We better do it fast," Spike said. "This vampire thing's making me nervous. Grandma says it's actually possible to get bitten and not even know it."

"Creepy," said Billy, rubbing his neck.

Reaching over to the wall, Spike pushed a thumb tack into the vampire poster he had recently purchased at the video store. "This is to remind us of the enemy we're up against," he said.

"Forget the poster," Emily said as she unwrapped her ham sandwich with lettuce, sliced tomatoes, and cheese. "The important thing is to figure out what to do."

"Isn't there a cure for this or some sort of pill that gets rid of the vampire in Violetta?" asked Tulu, munching on her peanut butter and jelly sandwich. "Or maybe there's something we can do to turn her back into a regular person."

"Violetta was *never* a regular person," said Emily.

Billy took a sip of his soda. "Regular or not, we need to cure her for her own sake. And ours, too," he added.

Spike brushed his hair out of his eyes. "Grandma says there *are* a couple of ways to get rid of vampires, but the problem is, they're pretty . . ." Spike hesitated, searching for the right word. "They're a bit . . . gross."

"Like what?" asked Frankie.

"Well," said Spike. "You can hammer a wooden stake through the vampire's heart. Or you can cut off its head with a grave digger's shovel."

"Eeek!" cried Tulu as she watched the red jelly ooze out of her sandwich.

"On the other hand," said Spike thoughtfully, "there are several things you can do to get rid of a werewolf that aren't so bad. Maybe a werewolf cure would work on a vampire. After all, they *are* related."

"Why not?" said Billy.

"There's one thing we could try," said Spike thoughtfully. "It's a little complicated, but maybe we can pull it off."

"Shoot!" said Billy.

Shocked, Tulu turned to him, her eyes wide with fear. "We can't *shoot* Violetta," she said.

Billy laughed. "I didn't mean to *shoot* her. I was just telling Spike to go ahead and tell us the plan."

Tulu nodded. "What is it, then?" she asked, turning back to Spike.

"It goes this way," Spike said. "We take Violetta to an isolated spot in the country. When we get there, we draw a circle seven feet wide and put the vampire inside. Then three people dressed in white robes dance around to make the vampire go away."

Tulu's eyes sparkled. "I like that!" she said. "I've been taking dancing lessons and this can be my first performance in public."

Billy wrote down antivampire directions in the official club notebook. Then he said, "What's next?"

"You take a potion made of vinegar and tar. Billy, I bet you can make that," Spike said. "And then you pour the potion around the vampire and shout to the vampire part of the person to go away and never come back. If it works for a werewolf, it should work for a vampire."

"But how are we going to get Violetta to the country?" Billy asked.

Spike paused. "That *is* a problem. With her vampire powers, she could probably tell we were trying to trick her."

"Why don't we use a stand-in?" Emily suggested, "or an object that belongs to her."

"Why not?" Billy asked. "It worked in *The Swamp Monster Returns*, when they cast a long distance spell on the Glob from the Lost Lagoon."

Spike shrugged. "It's worth a try," he said. "But who's going to get a lock of Violetta's hair or something that belongs to her?"

Emily held up her hand and smiled. "Leave that up to me," she said mysteriously.

Frankie looked at Billy. "Can you write a poem for the ceremony?"

Billy nodded, then wrote an official reminder in the club notebook.

"That settles it, then," said Frankie. "Billy reads a poem and the rest of us are dancers."

Spike shook his head hard. "No way," he said. "You're not going to catch me dressed up in a white gown dancing around with you and Tulu and Emily."

"Why not?" asked Tulu. "We're good dancers."

Spike clenched his teeth and squared his jaw. "You actually want *me* to deck myself out in a dress and dance around in a circle like some kind of a weirdo?"

"It's for the good of all of us," said Billy. "The more dancers, the more powerful the spell will be."

"If you wear a dress, then I'll wear one," Spike said, looking directly at Billy. "If you've got the nerve, I've got the nerve."

"Yea!" cried Tulu, her eyes glittering with anticipation. "I love dances!"

"Great," said Frankie. "So where are we going to do this? It has to be someplace that looks like country."

"A cemetery's probably best," said Billy. "That's where ghouls live when they rise from the dead."

"How about Spring Lawn?" said Emily. "Even if it *is* a little run down, it's only five blocks away and it has some trees, so it does look a little bit like country."

"Let's do it during the day," said Tulu. "I don't want to visit a cemetery at night."

"I don't know," said Billy, shaking his head. "Dark is better. Who ever heard of magic taking place at lunchtime?"

"Not *too* dark," said Tulu.

"Then let's do it *close* to dark, like after dinner," Emily said. "It stays light till almost nine."

Everyone agreed.

"Tomorrow night's the night," said Spike as he stood up and started to climb down the ladder.

"Right," said Emily. "And . . . don't forget to bring sheets."

"Yeah," said Billy.

"How could I forget?" Spike muttered.

Frankie squinted her eyes. "Violetta Epstein's vampire days are definitely numbered," she said.

Tulu glanced out the attic window. Suddenly her mouth fell open. "Look!" she cried, pointing to the ground below. "It's them!"

The group watched as Violetta ran toward Spike's front porch and stuck an envelope under a flower pot. Scurrying back to Bunny, both girls took off down the street. In a flash, they were gone.

"Let's go!" yelled Spike.

"Meeting adjourned!" Frankie cried out as the kids scrambled down the ladder, down the stairs, and out the front door.

"There!" Emily said, pointing.

Bending down, Billy picked up a violet envelope. "It's for you," he said, handing it to Spike.

"Pew!" said Spike. "It stinks!"

Frankie sniffed the air. "That's passion-flower perfume," she snickered. "Violetta's really got a thing for you."

Spike stared at the envelope as if it were the rattlesnake he almost stepped on.

"Aren't you going to open it?" Billy asked.

As if he were moving in slow motion, Spike nodded. Then he opened the envelope. With a trembling hand, he unfolded the letter. The kids crowded around him as he read.

> Dear Spike,
>
> I just wanted to tell you that I want to be your friend. Even more than your friend. I want us to be like Johnny and Belinda. Maybe we can meet alone sometime and go to the movies or something. I'd like that. Would you? Please answer this soon. I look forward to hearing from you.
>
> Eternally yours,
> Violetta

"Look out," said Billy. "She wants to get you alone."

Frankie took a deep breath. "And she signed the letter 'eternally yours.'"

Emily's freckled face turned pale. "As in together for all eternity . . . like Johnny and Belinda."

CHAPTER SIX

Spike paced up and down in front of his house as he waited for the members of the Canal Street Club to arrive. Glancing impatiently at his watch, he thought, I wonder what's keeping them? I've talked to everyone about the final plans at least twice today.

"Yo, Spike!" Billy called out as he rounded the corner carrying a sheet in one hand and a can of black goo in the other.

Spike smiled and waved. "Is that the potion?" he asked when Billy arrived.

"Yep. I got some tar from the street repair crew over on Tuttle Road. They told me the tar would get too hard to stir in the vinegar, so they gave me something called naptha to mix with the potion to make it stay soft."

"Hey, guys," Emily said as she walked over to the group.

Just then Frankie and Tulu arrived from the other end of the block. Tulu wore her sheet wrapped around her shoulders, but Frankie wore black.

"Why are you wearing *that?*" Spike asked Frankie.

Frankie looked down and smoothed the folds in her long cape. "Oh . . . this ole thing?" she asked, twirling once to show how the cape flared gracefully around her. "When I saw my vampire costume in the closet, I knew it would make the perfect dramatic statement."

"Dramatic statement about what?" asked Spike.

Frankie tossed her blond hair to the side. "About getting rid of the vampire. What else?" she asked.

Emily looked at Spike and asked, "So where's your sheet?"

Rolling his eyes, Spike jerked his head toward his house where a pink-and-white sheet lay folded over the fence. "I couldn't find an all-white one," he said sheepishly.

"Neither could I," said Tulu, holding out her sheet decorated with Eiffel towers and French cafés. Frankie and Tulu's mother was born in France.

"What part of Violetta are we going to use in the ceremony?" Billy asked.

Emily smiled. "We'll pick it up on the way to the cemetery," she said.

"So let's get this show on the road," Frankie said. "We promised we'd be home by before nine."

Sticking close together, the kids crossed Pacific Avenue and walked toward the cemetery along the Grand Canal. Everything seemed quiet and peaceful. Kids canoed lazily toward home as mother ducks gave their fuzzy brown-and-yellow babies swimming lessons. Across the canal a family sat out on their deck and ate dinner. Next door, their neighbors played croquet with some friends.

"Just think," said Spike, "if we fail in our mission, in a few weeks all these people could be turned into vampires."

"We'll be heroes and nobody will ever even know it," Spike said wistfully.

Just as the kids passed Austin Avenue, Emily said, "We have to make a quick detour past Violetta's house."

"Shhh!" Emily said as the group approached the Epstein's house. Dead cactus still decorated the yard. And all the dolls still sat on Mr. Epstein's needlepoint pillows on the front-porch swing.

"I'll be right back," Emily whispered.

In spite of themselves, the kids started to giggle as Emily dashed through the gate and up the walk to the front porch. Wasting no time, she grabbed the first doll she put her hands on and ran back down the walk to the street.

"Ta-da!" she cried in a hushed voice as she held up Violetta Epstein's surfer doll. She wore a tiny blue-and-white bikini, and the doll's long blond hair waved and curled down to its knees.

"Rhurrmph!" Billy snorted. "You're gonna use *that* as a substitute for a vampire?"

"Why not?" said Emily with a grin.

"Yeah, why not?" said Spike, suddenly bursting into laughter.

"Shhh!" Tulu said, giggling.

The Canal Street kids had almost reached their destination when Spike suddenly held up his hand.

"Stop!" he commanded in a hushed whisper. Then he pointed toward the front of Spring Lawn Cemetery. They watched in silence as Pops Papadopoulos, the caretaker, walked alongside the wrought-iron fence toward the old-fashioned iron gate at the front entrance to the cemetery.

"He's gonna lock us out!" said Tulu with more relief in her voice than she intended.

"No sweat," said Billy. "I've squeezed between the bars of the fence lots of times."

Frankie, Spike, Emily, Tulu, and Billy stood in the shadows of a hibiscus bush until Pops threaded the chain around the bars of the gate and fence, and secured it with a padlock. Then he walked slowly to the little wooden guardhouse at the back of the grounds.

"I hope he stays there," said Emily.

As if her wish were granted, she watched Pops through the window as he settled into an easy chair, pointed his remote control, and turned on the television.

"This way," Billy whispered, motioning the kids to follow him.

One by one Emily, Spike, Frankie, Tulu, and Billy slipped between the iron bars of the high fence and stepped into the cemetery.

"Shhhh!" hissed Frankie as they tiptoed past the guardhouse. Then they walked slowly and silently up the low hill, winding in and out of old gravestones.

"Look!" said Tulu. She stood transfixed in front of a weathered gray stone marker as tears sprung to her eyes. "He was only four years old."

The kids stopped and read the words that time and weather had almost erased.

HERE LIES WEE WILLY

WHO BROUGHT US SUCH JOY.

LONG MAY HE REST.

SLEEP TIGHT, WILLY BOY.

IN MEMORY OF WILLY AMES 1891–1895

"Creepy," whispered Billy.

"Sad," said Frankie.

Emily put her hand on Tulu's shoulder.

Frankie looked toward the top of the hill. "There," she said in a low voice, pointing to a small clearing that was partially shielded from the guardhouse by overgrown bushes and a weeping willow tree.

"Looks like a good place to me," Emily said as they walked silently to the clearing.

"This is it," said Billy.

"Are you sure it's safe?" asked Tulu, looking around her. As the sun moved lower in the sky, the trees and bushes and gravestones cast long eerie shadows across the grass.

"Don't be such a scaredy cat," Spike said to Tulu. "We'll take care of you. You don't have a thing to worry about."

"Okay, kids," Frankie said. "It's time to put on your costumes."

Frankie slipped fake vampire fangs over her teeth. Emily helped Tulu secure her sheet around her shoulders like a cape. Pictures of French cafés and Eiffel towers cascaded in soft waves behind her as she walked. Then Emily took her own sheet and tied it around one shoulder like a Greek toga. Billy wrapped his sheet around his shoulders as he stared sheepishly at the ground.

Grumbling rebelliously, Spike placed his pink-and-white sheet around his shoulders, treating it as if it were a boa constrictor. Then he pulled a piece of string from his back pocket and unwound it. He tied a fat piece of chalk to one end and a stick to the other, then jammed the stick in the dirt. Instructing Billy to hold on to the stick, Spike pulled the string tight and drew a crude circle on the dew-damp grass.

"Okay," Spike said to Emily. "Put the doll down right there in the middle of the circle."

Emily stood the doll in the middle of the circle,

making certain she was secure and wouldn't topple over halfway through the ceremony. Then Billy began to chant a funeral march, "dum dum de dum dum de dum de dum de dum," as he opened his can of potion. Taking a stick, he pulled out a glob of gooey black liquid.

"Whew! That stuff's nasty!" cried Frankie as she scrunched her face in a tight ball and backed away from the open can.

"Can't be helped," said Billy as he spread the tar and vinegar and naptha in a circle around Violetta's doll. "I mixed a little garlic into the potion, just to make sure."

Suddenly Tulu's eyes popped open wide. "Did you hear that?" she gasped.

"What?" asked Emily.

"I heard a noise," she said. "Coming from 'Here lies Wee Willy.'"

"Don't be silly, Tulu," Spike said, looking down at his pink-and-white skirt. "Let's just get this thing over with." He paused, then asked, "Everybody ready?"

Billy stood up and reached into his pocket. Pulling out a sheet of lined paper, he nodded and said, "Yes." Then Emily began to clap rhythmically as Frankie swayed dramatically back and forth to the beat. Concentrating on form and style, Tulu raised her hands and did a swift pirouette. She'd been taking dancing lessons for almost a year and had looked forward to this dance, her first public recital.

"Move it, Spike," said Emily as she took his hand and tugged him toward the circle. "We need *all* the dancers! How can you expect this antivampire spell to work if you're not doing your part?"

Reluctantly getting into the spirit of the ceremony, Spike started to hip-hop around the circle, his hands flapping wildly up and down, up and down. Twirling and whirling, Tulu danced around the doll as Emily and Frankie turned and skipped close behind. Prancing and swaying, the kids danced faster and wilder as Billy began the poem he called "Ode to a Dead Vampire."

"What do you do for a vampire's curse?
You can't call the doctor. You can't call the nurse.

"You can't find the lamps where the genies dwell,
So what do you do that will break the spell?

"You dance the dance right along with me.
With a hip-hop step, Violetta's free!"

Emily clapped her hands in time with Billy's poem as Spike accompanied him with cachoo-cachoo-cachoo sounds. The antivampire dancers moved faster and faster around the circle hopping, swaying, and twirling to the rhythm of Billy's ode.

"Who do the voo-do that you do so well?
Who do the chants that will soon break the spell?

"Hey nonnie nonnie yippie tie yie yea!
The vam-pi-res went that-a-way."

As Billy's voice faded away on the soft summer air, he picked up a stick and began to beat out the rhythm on the side of his potion can as his friends pranced around the doll. The bikinied doll stood still in the circle of vinegar and tar, her long, blond tresses occasionally catching the light of a passing car. Without warning, a strange sound drifted from behind the weeping willow tree.

"Woooooo . . . wooooo . . ."

Coming to a sudden halt, the dancers stared in the direction of the noise.

"Woooooo . . . wooooo . . ."

Spike's eyes bugged open and his mouth gaped wide. "It's a gggghost," he choked, gripping his pink-and-white sheet for protection.

Holding fast to his poem, Billy's hand began to shake. Unable to move, Emily stood next to him.

Then from the opposite direction, another chilling voice drifted slowly toward the astounded children. "Wooooo . . . wooooo . . . wooo."

Frankie gasped. "There are two ghosts!"

"Help," Tulu whimpered, grabbing her sister's hand.

"Holy cow," Billy croaked.

"Oooooooo . . . youuuu . . ." wailed the voice from behind them.

Spike gulped. "They're after us!"

"Eeek!" shrieked Tulu, throwing her arms around Frankie's waist and burying her face in her sheet.

"Holy coooow . . ." Emily whispered.

"Woooo . . . wooooooo." the ghost moaned. "Wooooo . . ."

"Ohhhhhhh . . . ooooooo," the other ghost groaned.

"Run!" Spike yelled. "Run!"

"WHEEE! WHEEEEE!!!" A shrill whistle split the evening silence. Everyone, including the ghost, stopped dead in their tracks.

"WHEEEWHEEEWHEEE!"

Looking down the hill, the Canal Street kids watched as Pops Papadopoulos walked briskly toward them. He was accompanied by two angry policemen.

"Uh-oh," said Spike. "Now we're *really* in for it."

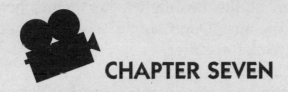

CHAPTER SEVEN

Without breaking stride, Pops Papadopoulos walked over to the Canal Street kids, followed by two policemen. "Okay," said Pops. "The game's over."

Spike's pink-and-white sheet hung limply from one shoulder as he looked up at Pops and the police officers. "Are—are we in trouble?" he stammered.

"I bet you can figure that out by the time we get to the police station," said the taller of the two officers.

"Come along quietly," said the other policeman.

"But what about the ghosts?" cried Tulu.

"Ghosts?" asked the second officer. "There's no such thing as ghosts."

"But we heard them! They were right over there." Tulu pointed toward the willow tree with her right hand and with her left, pointed at Wee Willy.

Officers Kravitz and Watson shined their flashlights on the tree and the gravestone. "If there's anyone there, you'd better come out," said Officer Kravitz.

From behind Wee Willy, Bunny Bigalow stepped

into the beam of the flashlights, her hands held delicately in the air. "Don't shoot," she squeaked. "Don't shoot Violetta, either."

"Violetta?" growled Frankie.

"It is I," Violetta said, waving her hand from behind the willow tree. "Woooo . . . wooooooo . . ."

Frankie put her hands on her hips as Violetta stepped into the light. "What are you two doing here?" she demanded.

"Scaring you," said Violetta. "And you'll have to admit, Frankie Stevens, I gave an Academy Award performance."

"I helped!" said Bunny, scurrying over to her friend. "I helped a lot."

"Spare me," said Frankie.

"Cut the chatter, kids," Officer Watson said. "You're all trespassing on private property and that means you are all under arrest."

"Under arrest!" squealed Bunny.

"Me?" cried Violetta. "You can't arrest me. I'm innocent!"

"Tell it to the judge," snorted Officer Kravitz.

"Innocent? Right!" mumbled Emily.

Twenty minutes later, Mr. and Mrs. Stevens burst through the doors of the police station, followed closely by Billy Lopez's father. The Canal Street kids, along with Bunny and Violetta, sat on a bench next to the bulletin board filled with wanted posters.

"Francesca! Louisa!" cried Mrs. Stevens in her heavy French accent. "What ees happening?"

"Billy?" said Mr. Lopez, clearly agitated. "What is all this about?"

Mr. Stevens walked over to the desk sergeant.

"What happened, officer?" asked Mr. Stevens. His brow wrinkled with concern.

"Well, sir, we found them in Spring Lawn Cemetery. We're not quite sure what they were up to."

"In the cemetery!" Mr. Lopez said. "What were they doing there?"

The police officer shrugged. "Beats me!" he said, holding up the doll. "All I know is that they were moaning like ghosts and dancing around this doll."

"My doll!" Violetta cried. "Bunny and I saw them kidnap her and we followed them." She snatched the doll from the officer's hand. After quickly inspecting her bikinied blond, she added, "Thank goodness you're all right."

"We were going to give your silly ole doll back," said Billy.

"We just borrowed it to get rid of the vampire," said Spike.

Just then, Mr. and Mrs. Epstein entered the station.

"What's going on here?" asked Mr. Epstein.

"Mommy!" Violetta cried out, the pink bow in

her hair bobbing up and down. "Daddy! Get me out of here! There are vampires in this place!"

"*You're* the vampire!" cried Tulu with a trembling voice as she pointed at Violetta.

"The what?" asked Mrs. Epstein.

Mrs. Stevens shook her head back and forth. "The vampeere," she said with a shrug.

"*Who's* a vampire?" asked the desk sergeant.

Tulu, Spike, Emily, Billy, and Frankie all pointed their fingers at Violetta. "*She* is!" they cried.

Violetta's eyes opened so wide that Spike thought they were going to pop out of her skull. "I am *not* a vampire!" she screamed. "I'm not, I'm not, I'm not!" she repeated, stomping her foot angrily.

In the middle of the commotion, Mr. and Mrs. Piranna walked into the police station.

"Spike?" said Grandpa Piranna. "What has happened? Why did the police call us?" he asked.

Just then, Mrs. Piranna caught sight of Mr. Papadopoulos.

"Pops!" she cried, amazed to find herself standing next to her old friend. The police station turned silent, as everyone watched Mrs. Piranna and Mr. Papadopoulos. Mrs. Piranna touched Spike on his shoulder. "This is my grandson, Spike."

"That's also the young hooligan who was running around my cemetery dressed in a pink-and-white sheet," Mr. Papadopoulos said grumpily.

Mrs. Piranna stepped backwards and examined

her friend carefully. "My grandson dancing at a cemetery in a pink-and-white sheet?" she asked with astonishment. "Have you been sick recently?"

Mr. Papadopoulos scratched his head. "I was just fine until this evening," he said. "That's when I found these kids up on Heaven's Gate Hill dancing around a doll."

"A doll!" said Mr. Piranna. "Spike has a doll?"

At that moment, Dr. and Mrs. Anderson entered the police station along with the Bigalows.

"Mommy!" cried Bunny. "Daddy!"

The Andersons took one look at their frightened daughter sitting on the bench. Mrs. Anderson went immediately to Emily and gave her a hug while Dr. Anderson walked straight to the desk sergeant. "What's going on here, officer?" he asked.

The desk sergeant shook his head. "That's just what Officers Kravitz, Watson, and I were trying to determine," he said.

"Leave it to me," said Dr. Anderson, walking over to the kids. The policemen followed close behind. "Now," said Dr. Anderson in his most authoritative tone, "Frankie, since you're president of the Canal Street Club, why don't you tell us what happened."

Frankie stood up and cleared her voice. "We were only doing a magic dance to get rid of the vampire."

Dr. Anderson stepped back in surprise. "The vampire?" he asked. "What vampire?"

Frankie took a deep breath. "I don't quite know how to explain it," she said. "All I can tell you is that Violetta Epstein is a vampire."

Violetta popped off the bench like someone had stuck a pin in her rear. "Don't you dare call me that!" she shrieked.

"Pipe down, calm down, and sit down, Miss," said Officer Kravitz. "We're trying to get some information here."

Her face red with fury, Violetta sat back on the bench.

Dr. Anderson took a deep breath. "What ever in the world made you think this young lady is a vampire?"

"We don't *think* she's a vampire," Frankie said. "We have proof."

"Proof? What proof?" asked Officer Watson.

Frankie looked at Emily. "Why don't you tell them what you and Billy saw?" she said.

Emily stood up. "Well," she said. "Billy and I were walking past the Epstein's the other evening. It was just turning dark and all of a sudden a huge flock of bats flew past us."

"And everybody knows that vampires turn into bats at night," added Tulu.

"But those are *my* bats!" said Mr. Epstein. "I have a bat house behind my garage. The bats hang out there—so to speak, heh, heh—all day long, and then they go out at night and hunt."

"That's when they hunt for blood to suck," said Tulu.

"No, dear, these are fruit bats and they eat insects. As a matter of fact, I'm looking for a new home for them. I don't really have time for them now that I've become involved with searching for the treasure Captain Henderson was supposed to have buried in this area over a hundred and fifty years ago."

"Buried treasure?" asked Spike with undisguised excitement.

Billy's eyes lit up. "You're going to give away your bats?"

"A real treasure!" said Tulu. "In our very own neighborhood?"

"Quiet!" said Officer Kravitz. Then he turned to Emily. "Are you satisfied now, Miss? Do you understand that the Epstein's bats are just regular fruit bats?"

Emily looked at the floor and nodded her head. "If you say so, sir," she said.

"But what about the mirror?" asked Spike. "That's heavy duty proof of vampirism." Then he told everyone about how Violetta didn't have a reflection.

Mr. Lopez stepped forward. "I think can explain that," he said. "That was probably a special-effects mirror built for the vampire cowboy movie. There are two different reflectors behind the mirror. One functions as a regular mirror and the other half reflects the image away from the viewer."

"Oh," said Billy sheepishly. "Special effects . . . I should have thought of that."

"Oh . . ." said Frankie, Emily, Spike, and Tulu in unison.

"But what about the garlic?" Billy asked. "Violetta hates garlic. So do vampires."

Mrs. Epstein stepped forward. "All the Epstein women hate garlic," she said indignantly. "It disagrees with our delicate stomachs. Right, Violetta, dear?"

Violetta nodded vigorously.

Frankie looked at the policemen and shrugged. "As president of the Canal Street Club, I want to tell you officially that we didn't mean any harm. We really didn't."

The desk sergeant looked at Mr. Papadopoulos and asked, "Sir? Do you intend to press charges against these kids?"

Mrs. Piranna looked at Mr. Papadopoulos and smiled her sweetest smile. "These children hold their club meetings in my home once a week," she said. "They're good kids, Pops."

"Well," Mr. Papadopoulos hesitated. Then he looked at the policemen and said, "Since these rascals are friends of my friend, and since they didn't damage any property and haven't made any trouble for me before, I'll drop the charges this time."

"Oh, Pops!" said Mrs. Piranna. "Thank you so much! This won't happen again." She looked at the Canal Street kids and said in a low, firm voice, "Will it children?"

"No, oh no!" the kids said, shaking their heads vigorously. "Never again." Tulu's pigtails bobbed back and forth and Emily's curls bounced up and down.

Clutching the doll to her chest, Violetta said, "Well, you better not call me a vampire again, or next time *I'll* press charges!"

"Now, Miss," said the police officer. "Like I said before. Just calm down. We all know there's no such thing as vampires."

Dr. Anderson smiled heartily. "Of course not. Vampires and other contemporary mythological creatures are just figments of an overactive preadolescent imagination," he said professionally.

"Right," said Mr. Lopez.

"Right," said all the other grown-ups, with the exception of Grandma Piranna.

"Of course there's no such thing as a vampire," agreed Mrs. Epstein, her long canine teeth glinting in the light.

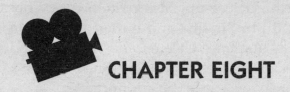

CHAPTER EIGHT

The Washington Wallop News from
George Washington Elementary School

EPSTEIN AND PIRANNA CAUGHT IN VAMPIRE EMBRACE
by Alex Harbottle

Crypt Riders in the Night, a movie starring some of our own Washington Elementary students, was presented in the school auditorium last Saturday night in an unforgettable fund-raising event.

Refreshments of fabulous jelly donuts, delicious brownies, and tangy fruit punch were provided free of charge by the PTA. Mrs. Epstein donated tofu cookies.

The plot of the movie was a little confusing, but there was lots of scary music and action and bloody teeth.

The appearance of WES students on screen drew lots of applause from the audience. Everyone's favorite scene was the one where Violetta Epstein and Spike Piranna were almost killed by a galloping horse.

In an exciting close-up, Ms. Epstein threw her arms around Mr. Piranna and buried her face in his neck. The audience cheered and whistled and whooped. During the commotion Spike Piranna was seen sneaking out of the auditorium.

Violetta Epstein was seen smiling. After the screening, she said, "I'm proud of my role in the movie. And I look forward to a career as a rich and famous movie star."

Brief glimpses of other WES students included Emily Anderson, Bunny Bigalow, Billy Lopez, Frankie Stevens, and her sister, Tulu.

The fundraising event made $179.50.

"That's the first time my name's ever been in the school newspaper," said Tulu.

"Me, too," said Spike glumly, staring at the headline.

"We were asked for lots of autographs," said Emily.

The Canal Street Club members stood outside the Lopez home, admiring Billy's new bat house.

"It's my first movie review," said Frankie, who had already pasted the article in her brand new scrapbook. "You know," she continued with a dreamy look, "there really is no business like show business."

Her friends smiled and waited for the bats to come out.